GUTSY Asian

Authors: Shera Fadzlin and Safiyya Suhaimi | Illustrator: Fatini Mohamad

First published in 2024 by Fuzzy Flamingo
Copyright © Shera Fadzlin and Safiyya Suhaimi 2024

Shera Fadzlin and Safiyya Suhaimi have asserted their right to be identified as the authors of this Work in accordance with the Copyright, Designs and Patents Act 1988.

ISBN: 978-1-7390943-8-6

All rights reserved.
No part of this publication may be reproduced, stored in a retrieval system, or transmitted in any form or by any means, electronic, mechanical, photocopying, recording or otherwise, without the prior permission of the copyright owner.

Editing and design by Fuzzy Flamingo
www.fuzzyflamingo.co.uk

A catalogue for this book is available from the British Library.

Contents

Foreword	v
Chien-Shiung Wu, China	1
Raden Adjeng Kartini, Indonesia	2
Yu Gwan-Sun, South Korea	5
Anna May Wong, China	6
Savitribai Phule, India	8
Yamamoto Yaeko, Japan	10
Nguyễn Thị Định, Vietnam	12
Shamsiah Fakeh, Malaysia	14
Asma Khan, India	16
Michelle Yeoh, Malaysia	18
Glossary	20
About the Authors	22

To all the mothers and daughters of Asian descent who stay connected to their roots while embracing diverse cultures wherever they live and striving to do things differently

Foreword

We embark on a journey to discover the tales of extraordinary Asian women who have long been hidden in the shadows of history. This collection is crafted with the intention to create awareness among children, both in general and particularly those of Asian descent. Our goal is to spark interest, fuel a passion for learning, and inspire the minds of tomorrow through the empowering stories of unsung heroines.

In the vast tapestry of human history, there exist stories of remarkable Asian women whose achievements have often been overlooked or overshadowed. These heroines, both from times long past and the present day, are the champions who have shaped the world with their courage, intelligence, and resilience. It is time to bring their tales to the forefront, to celebrate the strength and determination that defines them.

These are not stories of damsels in distress waiting to be rescued, but tales of bold, independent, and driven individuals who have carved their paths in the face of adversity. Through their journeys, we aim to showcase the vibrant tapestry of strength, equality, and empowerment. Whether you are a third-generation explorer or a curious soul seeking the roots of your identity, these stories invite you to feel pride in your heritage.

Parents, too, will find within these pages a channel to connect with their children, a means to introduce a vibrant history and heritage that has not been lost. As you read together, these stories become more than just words on paper – they become threads that weave the fabric of shared identity and cultural pride.

CHIEN SHIUNG WU

Chien-Shiung Wu was born in a little town near Shanghai, China. She was bright and clever and excelled in mathematics. She attended a school set up by her father, a **revolutionary** who fought for women's rights. He decided to start a school to educate girls. Her father always motivated her to ignore obstacles and reminded her, "Just put your head down and keep walking forward."

Her journey as an accomplished physicist was not as straightforward. She switched **majors** from mathematics to **physics**. Having done research in universities in China, she was encouraged to apply for a **PhD** abroad. In 1936, she decided to move to the US to study at the University of California, Berkeley.

Upon completing her **PhD**, Chien-Shiung and her husband moved to the East Coast and later accepted an offer from Princeton University as the first female **instructor** ever hired to join the **physics** faculty.

Dr Wu was involved in numerous monumental studies at Columbia University, including the Manhattan Project which produced the first **nuclear weapon**. After that, she joined a two-man team of physicists to **disprove** the **Law of Parity.** This success led to the 1957 **Nobel Prize** for the two male **physicists**; however, Dr Wu was excluded.

Aware of the **gender-based injustice**, she spoke out against **gender discrimination** at a **symposium** at the Massachusetts Institute of Technology in 1964. "I wonder whether the tiny atoms and nuclei, or the mathematical symbols, or the DNA molecules have any preference for either **masculine** or feminine treatment?" she asked her audience, to which they applauded.

In 1978 her role in disproving the Law of Parity was finally honoured when she was awarded the **inaugural** Wolf Prize.

Dr Wu is the author of the book Beta Decay, which is now considered standard reading for nuclear physicists. In 1995, four fellow physicists founded the Wu Chien-Shiung Education **Foundation** in Taiwan which aimed to provide scholarships to aspiring young scientists. A huge advocate for promoting girls and STEM (science, technology, engineering, and mathematics), a supporter of this cause and later a role model for young women scientists everywhere, and in 1998, Wu was inducted into the American National Women's Hall of Fame. Chien Shiung Wu's story is a reminder that determination, courage, and a passion for knowledge can change the world. She continues to inspire and pave the way for future scientists, leaving an indelible mark on the history of science and **equality**.

RADEN ADJENG KARTINI

Raden Adjeng Kartini was born on the 21st of April 1879. She was an Indonesian princess who lived in Jepara, Central Java. She was the fifth child and the second-eldest daughter in a family of eleven – including her half-siblings. She was born into a family with a strong intellectual tradition. Her father, Sosroningrat, was of **noble** descent and sent her to a Dutch elementary school, where she made new Dutch friends and learnt to speak the language.

Because she was born into an **aristocratic** Javanese family, her father removed her from school at the age of twelve. It was common practice among Javanese nobles that daughters were **secluded (pingit)** to prepare them for **wedlock**. During **seclusion**, girls were not allowed to leave their parents' house until they were married, after which the authority over them was transferred to their husbands.

During her seclusion, Kartini continued to **self-educate**. She was fluent in Dutch and acquired several Dutch pen pals. She thought it was unfair not to be able to continue her education, so she wrote letters to her Dutch friends and told them how she felt in the situation.

She was especially close to a Dutch girl by the name of Rosa Abendanon. Books, newspapers, and European magazines continued to feed Kartini's interest in Western and **feminist** thinking. She desired to improve the conditions of **indigenous** Indonesian women, who at the time had very **low social status**.

Later she married a man named Joyodiningrat, who was, the **Regency Chief** of Rembang. He had already married three women previously! Joyodiningrat agreed with her opinion on the lack of education for girls. She soon opened a school in Indonesia just for girls.

She passed away four days after giving birth to her only son. After her death, her sisters continued her **advocacy** of educating girls and women and a string of Kartini schools were **established** in her memory.

Kartini's letters were later published in a book and translated into English; *Letters of a Javanese Princess* and *From Darkness to Light*.

Today, Kartini is known as a prominent Indonesian activist who advocated for women's rights and female education. Her birth date, the 21st of April, has been **declared** as Kartini Day – an Indonesian national holiday to celebrate the strides she made for girls' freedom in Indonesia.

"Women's inequality is a result of being restricted from women's access to knowledge so that women become fools."

YU GWAN-SUN

Yu Gwan-Sun was born in 1902, in the village of Cheonan in South Korea. Yu Gwan-Sun grew up in a family that followed the teachings of the **Protestant** faith. She was brilliant and could remember passages from the Bible even after hearing them just once. Yu Gwan-Sun was lucky because she got to go to school and then to university. Back then, not many girls in Korea could go to university like she did.

When Yu Gwan-Sun was in school, she saw something important happening. People were peacefully protesting against the Japanese rulers who were in charge of Korea. This was called the Mansae Marches. Even though she was still a young schoolgirl, Yu Gwan-Sun joined these protests and went to demonstrations all over the country. She deeply felt that Korea should be **independent.**

When Yu Gwan-Sun was eighteen years old, her school said students shouldn't join protests. But she cared so much about her country that she decided to join the protests anyway, even though it was risky.

Yu Gwan-Sun was taken to jail by Japanese officers. They hurt her body, but they couldn't break her strong belief. She stayed in prison, and after a year, she and her inmates in jail began to shout for freedom, saying, "Long live Korean **independence**!" from their cells.

The officers tried to make Yu Gwan-Sun give up by hitting her and hurting her even more, but she didn't lose hope. They tortured her, even breaking her bones, but they couldn't break her **spirit**. After six months of shouting for freedom and enduring more pain, Yu Gwan-Sun sadly died in prison. Today, her strong spirit of **independence** lives on in the people of South Korea.

ANNA MAY WONG

Wong Liu Tsong was born on the 3rd of January 1905 in Chinatown Los Angeles where her father owned a laundromat, and her family lived in an integrated community of diverse people. When Wong Liu Tsong was a schoolgirl, she loved movies so much that she would often skip school and use her lunch money to go to the cinema. She would get close to the cameras and stare at glamorous movie stars and then rush home and recreate the scenes she watched in front of a mirror.

Wong and her older sister Lulu attended the California Street public elementary school but were teased and bullied because of their race. The game other children played was to gather around her sister and Anna and torment them. Wong lived during a **racially segregated** time. They later moved to the Chinese Mission School in Chinatown where they attended Chinese language classes and were accepted.

At the age of nine, she decided she wanted to become a movie star. She combined her English and Chinese names to create her stage name: Anna May Wong. When she was fourteen, without her father knowing, Anna asked her father's friend to introduce her to the assistant director of the movie "The Red Lantern". She got the casting call as an extra and was asked to carry a lantern in one of the scenes. This was her first but not her last movie. From then on, Anna continued to work as an extra in many movies while still attending school.

At age sixteen, Anna dropped out of high school to become an actress full-time. She was determined to give herself ten years to succeed. She did all kinds of movies from silent movies, radio, and stage to television. Anna appeared in over sixty movies throughout her career and was the first Asian-American actor to work in Hollywood, all this while facing racism and typecasting in an industry that restricted her from reaching her fullest potential.

In those years, the leading Chinese roles in Hollywood films were played by white actors heavily made up in yellow faces, dressed in very exaggerated costumes and had their eyes taped to look more Asian. Ghostly and terrifying! The roles she was offered were mostly demon roles where she dies at the end. Her acting impressed the audiences, but she had hoped Chinese and other Asian people would be represented worthily in movies.

Frustrated with the American movie industry, Anna left for Europe in 1928 at the age of twenty-three, where she started to get involved in stage work in London, Paris and Berlin. During this period, she moved between Europe and America frequently and starred in many plays, operas and films, including *The Flame of Love*, *Tschun Tschi* and *A Circle of Chalk* (with **Lawrence Olivier**).

Anna still received promises for leading roles in America, but upon her return, unfortunately, nothing had changed. They continued to cast her for supporting roles or stereotypical Asian roles either madame butterflies or dragon ladies. Anna reached a breaking point with these casting practices when she was passed over for the lead role in the movie Crimson City and was further insulted when she was told to teach the white lead how to use chopsticks.

Anna finally returned to America in the 1950s and became the first Asian-American to lead a US television show for her work on *The Gallery of Madame Liu-Tsong*. However, she died at the young age of fifty-six, after which the more recently established Asian-American Arts Awards and the Asian Fashion Designers group honoured her by naming their awards after her!

SAVITRIBAI PHULE

"Empower a woman, and you uplift an entire community."

On the 3rd of January 1831, in the beautiful land of India, a brave little girl named Savitribai was born. She lived in Naigaon, a small village where traditions said girls should marry early and not go to school.

Savitribai was just nine years old when she married a boy named Jyotirao Phule, who was only twelve. Even though Savitribai couldn't read or write, her husband saw her eagerness to learn and decided to teach her. Jyotirao saw her enthusiasm to learn and educate herself. He stood by her side as they embarked on a remarkable journey together.

In those times, India had a rigid **caste system**, a social hierarchy that divided people into different groups based on their birth. This was often determined by a person's job, social status, and even who they could marry. The upper **castes** enjoyed many privileges, while the lower **castes** faced discrimination and hardships. Women, especially those from lower **castes**, were denied education and treated unfairly. But Savitribai and Jyotirao worked hard and became leaders in **movements** to change these unfair rules. They fought to end the custom of untouchability and the **caste** system, and they wanted everyone to have the same rights.

Savitribai continued to have a thirst for knowledge. She passed exams and even went to teacher training. However, their passion for education led to them being isolated from their families and community. Savitribai and Jyotirao found support in their good friends, Usman and Fatima Sheikh, who shared their dreams of education for all.

Savitribai and Fatima went through teacher training together and graduated. They were on a mission to make a big change. Together, they opened the very first school for girls in Pune, India, right in Fatima's house. Setting up the first school for women in India teaching children from different castes, Savitribai became the first teacher and headmistress in India while Fatima became the first Muslim woman teacher of India.

Savitribai and Fatima Sheikh started teaching not only women but also people from lower castes who had been treated unfairly for far too long. However, not everyone was happy about this. The upper-caste people in Pune didn't like the idea of people from lower castes being educated. They threatened them, harassed them, and even humiliated them in front of others. Some people even threw cow dung and stones at Savitribai as she walked to the school. But none of these awful things stopped her.

Meanwhile, a night school was also opened by the Phule couple in 1855 for **agriculturists** and **labourers** so that they could work in the daytime and attend school at night.

Together, they opened a total of eighteen schools and even created a special place for pregnant women who had been victims of terrible crimes. This centre was a safe and secure place for these women to have their babies and protect them from harm. It saved the lives of both the mothers and their babies. Savitribai also worked hard to educate and empower young girls who had lost their husbands and campaigned against child marriage. She believed in giving these girls a chance to start anew.

Savitribai dedicated her entire life to promoting **social unity**, education, and women's empowerment. She played a crucial role in the fight for women's rights in India when the British ruled. Many people call her one of the very first Indian **feminists**. Her story reminds us that with determination and a caring heart, we can make a big difference in the world.

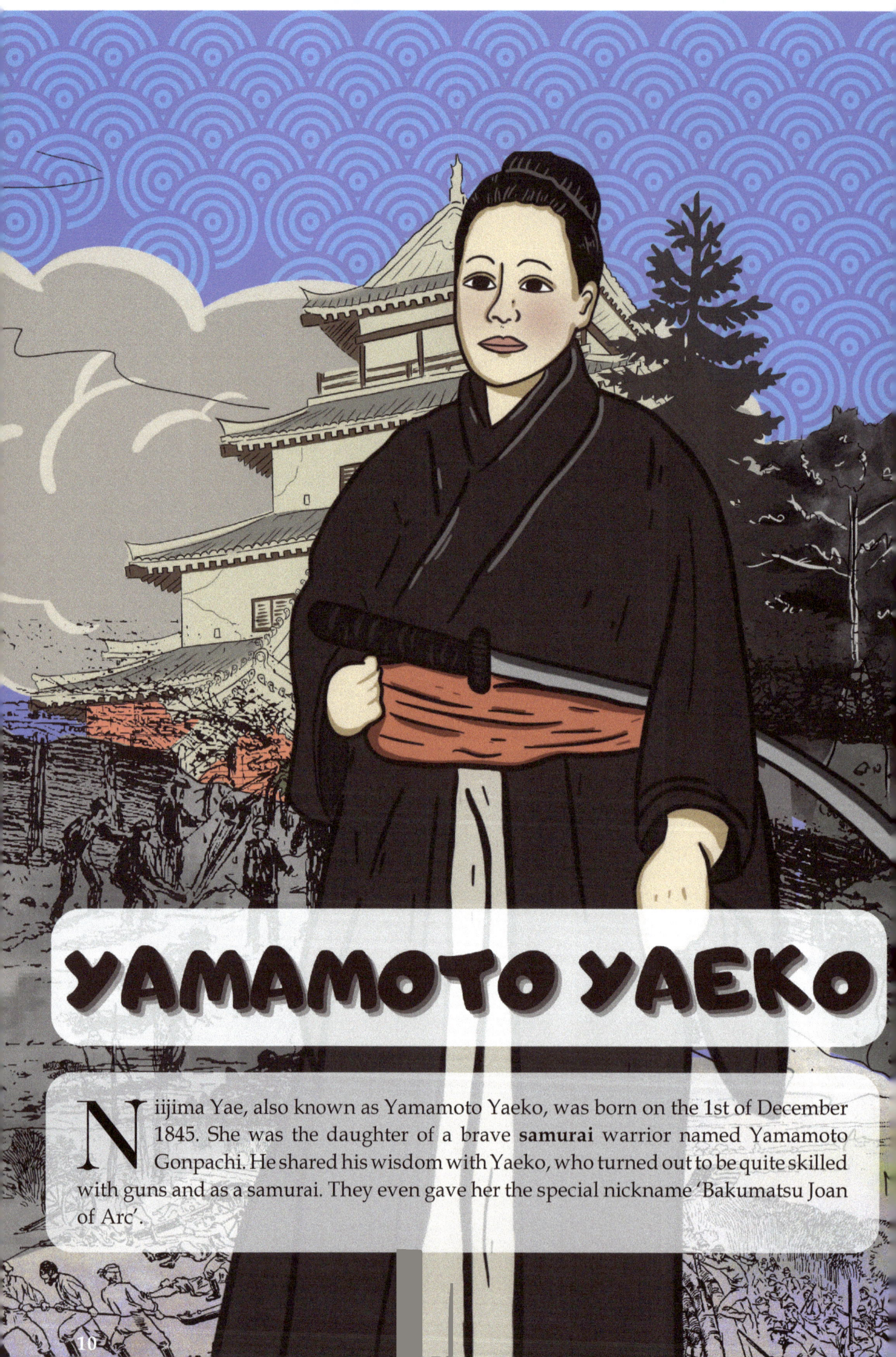

YAMAMOTO YAEKO

Niijima Yae, also known as Yamamoto Yaeko, was born on the 1st of December 1845. She was the daughter of a brave **samurai** warrior named Yamamoto Gonpachi. He shared his wisdom with Yaeko, who turned out to be quite skilled with guns and as a samurai. They even gave her the special nickname 'Bakumatsu Joan of Arc'.

Yaeko enlisted during the Battle of Aizu in the Boshin Wars in 1868. She joined the defence to protect one of the castles from the Meiji government and their friends. After Aizu surrendered, she had to hide in the Yonezawa Domain for one year while her then-husband was taken as prisoner. They later decided to go their separate ways.

While searching for her brother in Kyoto, Yaeko became a teacher at a girls' school. That's where she met Reverand Joseph Hardy Niijima, also known as Jō, who was an American-educated Christian **missionary** and a strong believer in women's rights. Jō was a former samurai who had spent a lot of time in the US. Together, they started a private school in Kyoto, which later became the Doshisha University.

Yaeko and Jō had a special relationship where they were equals and no one had more power than the other. Some people thought Yaeko wasn't a good wife because of this, but Jō loved Yaeko the way she was.

They were happily married for fourteen years until Jō died in 1890. Yaeko then left Doshisha University and joined the Japanese Red Cross where she became a chief nurse, leading a team of forty nurses during the Sino-Japanese War in 1894 and the Russo-Japanese War in 1905 to help nurse injured soldiers back to health.

Yaeko's selflessness and leadership in working with other women to help combat the barriers female nurses faced in the medical field, such as being treated unfairly by some male colleagues, led to her receiving two **Orders of the Precious Crown** for her services to the nursing profession.

To further honour her, the Japanese **Imperial House** bestowed upon her a shiny cup to say thank you for all her service to Japan; the first woman outside of the **Imperial House** to receive such an honour.

Many years later, in 1932 Yaeko passed away at the age of eighty-six. She was given a funeral sponsored by Doshisha University and was buried in Doshisha Cemetery. Her story reminds us that through leadership and goodwill, we can do amazing things to make the world more equal.

Nguyễn Thị Định was born in 1920, in a village called Ben Tre Province, Vietnam. She was one of ten children in a poor family of farmers. At the time she was born, Vietnam was a **colony** of France. She had an older brother who was part of a group of **revolutionaries** who fought to gain **independence** from French rule. Định admired her brother and started participating in anti-French resistance activities herself when she was sixteen years old.

She started by recruiting peasants to join the fight to gain Vietnam's **independence** from France before the start of World War II. In 1938, Nguyen married a fellow revolutionary, but the following year after their marriage, her husband was arrested by the French authorities shortly before she gave birth to a son. Despite this tragedy, Nguyen continued to be actively involved in the Viet Minh forces against the French and this led to her many arrests, but sadly her husband died in prison.

After the war, the country was divided into **Communist-led** North Vietnam and US-supported South Vietnam in 1954. Định remained in South Vietnam and led the resistance to the government of Ngô Đình Diệm. She became a founding member of the National Liberation Front (NLF) opposition group, which later became known as the Viet Cong. During the Vietnam War, Định organised several **anti-government** demonstrations by large groups of women, and became the highest-ranking female member of the Viet Cong!

She continued with her **activism** and was later elected chairwoman of the South Vietnam Women's Liberation Association, better known as the 'long-haired warriors'. These groups drew attraction from a lot of women as many were drawn to the promise of changes in the roles of women in society.

During her involvement with NLF, Định was an influential spokesperson, calling women to not only play a role in recruitment but to encourage adherence to a 'new morality' for NLF women popularised as the 'Three Postponements' campaign that sought to reform social customs to serve the war effort, urging the **postponement** of love, marriage and childbirth.

After the Vietnam War and the **reunification** of Vietnam, Định served on the central committee of the Vietnamese Communist Party and became the first female major general to serve the Vietnam People's Army as well as the first female vice-president of Vietnam. In 1967, she was awarded the **Lenin Peace Prize** and **posthumously** awarded the title Hero of the People's Armed Forces in 1995, three years after her death.

Dinh's memoir "No Other Road to Take" tells the story of a woman commander in the NLF who became a relatively famous figure in the United States because of her high rank and storied military career. Despite facing numerous hardships, she never gave up on her dream of a free and fair country. Nguyen Thi Dinh's story reminds us that with will and determination, we all can effect great change by standing by what we believe in.

Shamsiah Fakeh was born in 1924 in a village in Negeri Sembilan, Malaya (now known as Malaysia). Her family was very religious and quite poor.

During that time, women were not well educated and were only taught to do chores like cooking, sewing, and childcare, and were then married off at a young age. But Shamsiah was not an average Malay woman. She was very interested in politics, especially when the Japanese took over Malaysia.

In this period, the Japanese occupants in Malaysia were very harsh and cruel. The people in Malaysia, especially the Chinese community, suffered a lot. They had to severely **ration** their resources because there wasn't enough food, and prices were very high due to **hyperinflation.**

Shamsiah wanted to help her people by standing up to the Japanese. She became very vocal and spoke about her concerns publicly, and many political groups wanted her to join them.

Shamsiah believed that everyone should be treated equally. She saw that most people were poor while the British, who controlled Malaya, were rich and took Malaya's wealth back to Britain. This made her ideas about communism grow stronger. **Communism** is a belief that wealth and resources should be shared equally among all people. This **ideology** was popular and was founded by Karl Marx, a thinker from the nineteenth century, who believed in **equality** for everyone.

Shamsiah wanted to free her people from British control and make sure everyone shared the country's wealth. She became an important member of the Communist Party of Malaya and fought for **independence**. The British tried to stop communism and made strict regulations against it. So Shamsiah had to move to the jungle and fought with the Malayan People's Liberation Army for eight years.

In 1956, Shamsiah and her husband left for **exile** to China. They were later imprisoned in Indonesia for two years during a time when many communists were being arrested. They were freed in 1967 and stayed in China until 1994 when they were allowed to return to Malaysia.

Shamsiah wrote in her memoir, "I was just a woman fighting the British for my country's **independence** and the **emancipation** of women."

Shamsiah died in 2008, but her story is one of great courage and determination. She faced many hardships but never gave up on her dream of a free and fair country. Her bravery shows that anyone, no matter where they come from or what challenges they face, can make a difference in the world. Shamsiah's legacy inspires young girls to stand up for what they believe in and to fight for their dreams with courage and strength.

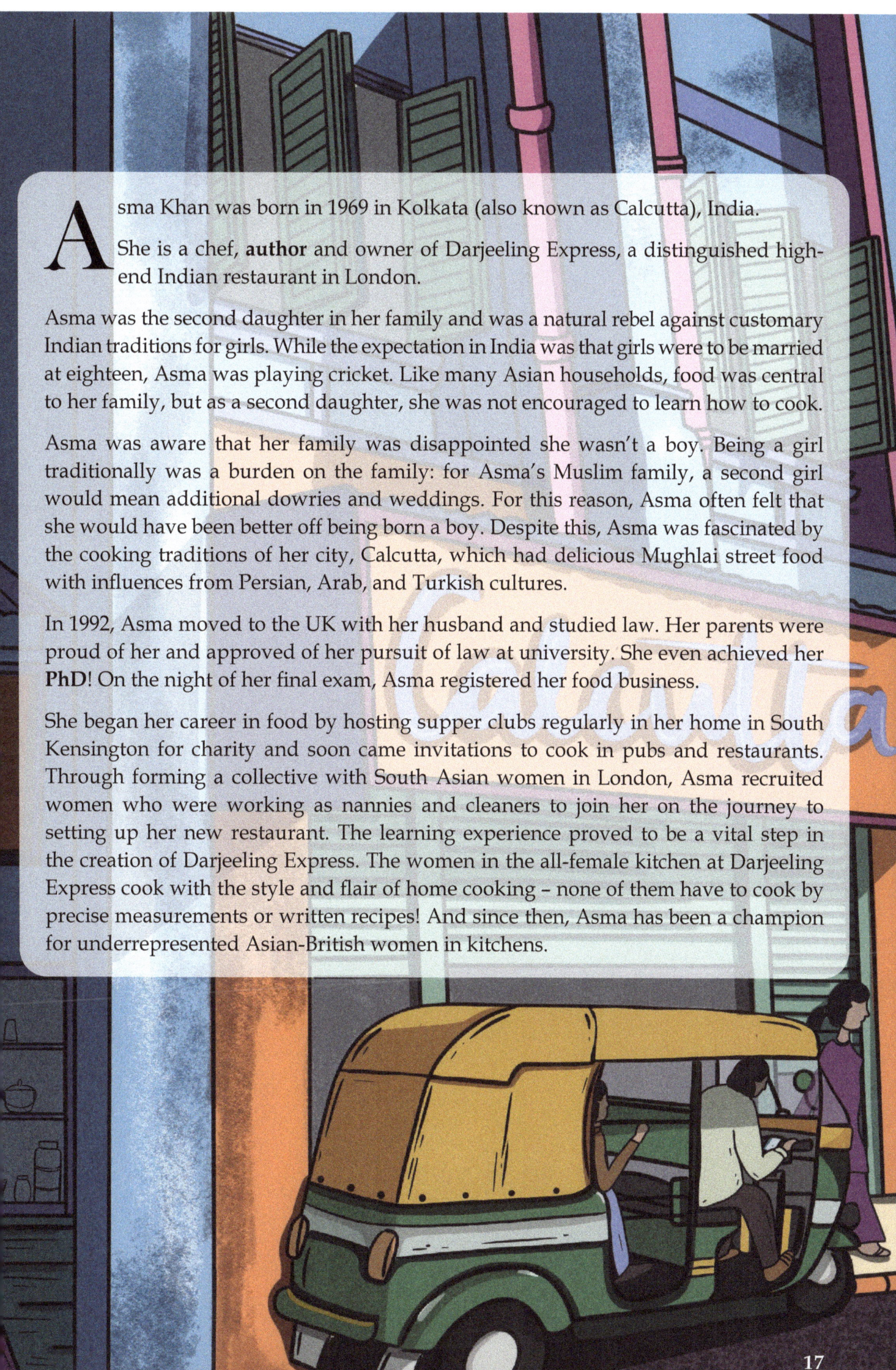

Asma Khan was born in 1969 in Kolkata (also known as Calcutta), India. She is a chef, **author** and owner of Darjeeling Express, a distinguished high-end Indian restaurant in London.

Asma was the second daughter in her family and was a natural rebel against customary Indian traditions for girls. While the expectation in India was that girls were to be married at eighteen, Asma was playing cricket. Like many Asian households, food was central to her family, but as a second daughter, she was not encouraged to learn how to cook.

Asma was aware that her family was disappointed she wasn't a boy. Being a girl traditionally was a burden on the family: for Asma's Muslim family, a second girl would mean additional dowries and weddings. For this reason, Asma often felt that she would have been better off being born a boy. Despite this, Asma was fascinated by the cooking traditions of her city, Calcutta, which had delicious Mughlai street food with influences from Persian, Arab, and Turkish cultures.

In 1992, Asma moved to the UK with her husband and studied law. Her parents were proud of her and approved of her pursuit of law at university. She even achieved her **PhD**! On the night of her final exam, Asma registered her food business.

She began her career in food by hosting supper clubs regularly in her home in South Kensington for charity and soon came invitations to cook in pubs and restaurants. Through forming a collective with South Asian women in London, Asma recruited women who were working as nannies and cleaners to join her on the journey to setting up her new restaurant. The learning experience proved to be a vital step in the creation of Darjeeling Express. The women in the all-female kitchen at Darjeeling Express cook with the style and flair of home cooking – none of them have to cook by precise measurements or written recipes! And since then, Asma has been a champion for underrepresented Asian-British women in kitchens.

Michelle Yeoh was born on the 6th of August 1962 in Ipoh, Malaysia. She had a special place in her heart for dreams and adventures. She grew up speaking English and a bit of Malaysian Cantonese. Her days were filled with laughter and fun, especially at the Ipoh Swimming Club near her home. She loved sports and was a national-level athlete in swimming, diving and squash. Her true dream, the one that twinkled in her eyes since she was just four years old, was to become a ballet dancer.

At the age of fifteen, Michelle moved with her parents to the UK. She went to a boarding school in Chester to get closer to her dream of being a dancer. Later, she was accepted at the Royal Academy of Dance in London, where she majored in ballet. But life had a surprise waiting for her. In her final year at the academy, Michelle faced a setback when she injured her spine, which put a pause on her dream of becoming a prima ballerina. Instead of giving up, Michelle considered opening her very own ballet school.

In 1982, Michelle earned her **BA** in Creative Arts with a minor in Drama. She didn't know it then, but her life was about to change in a big way. In the summer of 1983, her mother entered her in the 'Miss Malaysia' beauty pageant, and guess what? Michelle won! This unexpected victory opened doors to commercials and, soon after, the newly popular Hong Kong film industry.

Michelle was featured in many films. In her early movies, Michelle combined her love of sports and dance. These action scenes required Michelle to learn action choreography and perform all her own stunts! To prepare herself, Michelle would undergo intensive physical training. She began in films like *The Owl vs Bombo* and *Twinkle, Twinkle, and Lucky Stars*. She became the highest-paid actress in Asia and was famous for her stunts.

In 1992, she starred in *Police Story 3: Supercop* with Jackie Chan, among others. However, the physical challenges of her action roles sometimes reminded her of her old injuries.

Michelle's international breakout role was in the James Bond film *Tomorrow Never Dies* in 1997 as a Chinese agent alongside Bond. Michelle gained recognition for this role in Hollywood. While Hong Kong films gained more traction in the US, she continued to feature and star in its films rather than accept every offer from Hollywood. But what followed were some of her most notable works: *Crouching Tiger, Hidden Dragon* in 2000, which won four Academy Awards, and *Memoirs of a Geisha* in 2004.

In 2023, Michelle Yeoh made history by becoming the first Asian woman to win the Academy Award for Best Actress in a Leading Role at the Oscars for her outstanding performance in *Everything Everywhere All at Once*.

Michelle Yeoh's journey from a little girl in Ipoh to an international star shows that even when things seem tough, amazing things can still happen if you keep going. Her recognition as the first Asian woman to win the Academy Award for Best Actress proves that hard work and perseverance can break barriers.

Glossary

Activism: Working hard and campaigning to make big changes in society.
Advocacy: Supporting and speaking up for a cause or idea.
Agriculturists: People who work on farms growing crops and raising animals.
Anti-government: Not agreeing with or opposing the government.
Aristocratic: Belonging to a high social class; noble.
Author: A person who writes books, articles, or stories.
BA: Short for Bachelor of Arts, an undergraduate degree.
Caste system: A way of organizing people into different social groups based on birth, common in some countries.
Colony: A country or area controlled by another country.
Communism: A system where everything is shared equally and the government owns all property.
Communist-led: Controlled or guided by communist principles.
Declared: Officially announced something.
Disprove: Show that something is not true.
Emancipation: The act of freeing someone from control or unfair treatment.
Established: Something that has been around for a long time and is well-known.
Equality: Everyone has the same rights and opportunities.
Exile: Being forced to live away from your home country.
Feminist: Someone who believes in and supports equal rights for women and men.
Foundation: The basic idea or principle behind something.
Gender-based injustice: Unfair treatment of people because of their gender (whether they are male or female).
Gender discrimination: treating some people differently from others, in unfair ways because of gender.
Hyperinflation or inflation: Prices go up very fast, making money worth less.
Ideology: A set of ideas and beliefs about how things should be.
Imperial House: The family or group that rules an empire.
Inaugural: The first event in a series, like a first speech or ceremony.
Independent: Free from control by others; able to do things on your own.
Independence: Being free from control by others.
Indigenous: the first people to live in a place.
Instructor: A teacher.
Labourers: Workers, especially those who do physical work.

Law of parity: A rule in physics about how certain actions are the same even if they are reversed.
Lenin Peace Prize: An award given for promoting peace.
Low social status: Being in a lower position in society.
Major(s): the most important subject(s) one is studying at college or university.
Masculine or feminine: Traits or qualities that are traditionally linked to being male or female.
Missionary: Someone who goes to another place to teach their religion.
Movements: Large groups of people working together to achieve a goal.
Nobel Prize: This important award is given each year for achievements in areas like peace, literature, and science.
Noble: Belonging to a high-ranking social class.
Nuclear weapon: A very powerful bomb that uses nuclear reactions to create an explosion.
Orders of the Precious Crown: the highest Japanese honour for women.
PhD: A high-level college degree that involves a lot of research, an abbreviation of Doctor of Philosophy.
Physicist: A scientist who studies physics, the science of matter and energy.
Physics: The science that studies how things move and interact.
Posthumously: Something happening after a person has died.
Postponement: Delaying something to a later time.
Protestant: A member of a Christian church that separated from the Roman Catholic Church.
Racially segregated: When people are separated into different groups based on race.
Ration: A fixed amount of something that people are allowed to have, especially during a shortage.
Reunification: Bringing things or people back together after they have been separated.
Revolutionary(ies) (noun): a person who starts or supports a revolution – especially a political one.
Samurai: an ancient warrior in the Japanese military - similar to knights in the Medieval times.
Seclusion: the state of being private and away from other people.
Wedlock: old word used for the state of being married.

Shera was born in Malaysia and grew up in Kuala Lumpur until her late teens. She left for the UK to do her A levels and then studied law at Newcastle University. With an LLB (Hons), she came back to Kuala Lumpur to work as an in-house lawyer in a broadcasting station and later moved to the newsroom as a broadcast journalist. After a short-lived career, she went on to serve her tenure with an oil and gas multinational in PR and communications. After ten years, her family moved to the Middle East where she lived for eight years and worked as an expatriate in the field of education.

Shera now resides in the tranquil beauty of the English countryside. A multi-talented entrepreneur driven by a desire to share her passion for creativity and gastronomy with others, she has carved a unique niche for herself offering homecooked authentic Malaysian cuisine to nearby villages and nationwide. She occasionally runs cooking and batik painting workshops within her home; a celebration of community, connection and the simple joys of rural life.

With a deep personal journey of discovery and empowerment, she was inspired to develop the idea for this book along with her daughter Safiyya.

Safiyya was born in Kuala Lumpur and grew up in Muscat, Oman. She moved to the UK to attend boarding school at the age of thirteen, which presented its challenges for the first three years and resulted in emotionally arrested development. During this time, her parents went through a divorce, and lacking role models to navigate her through a tormenting adolescence, Safiyya found inspiration from the rich history of Asian women. Through her contributions to this book, she came to the realisation that feminine power can drive a change in narrative. Diversity and the sharing of stories of inspiring women allows us to recognise our potential as reflected by the innate creativity that flows between us. It removes the necessity for us to gather knowledge and wisdom clandestinely in forests, only to be accused of witchcraft. Safiyya hopes that *Gutsy Asian* is a beacon of empowerment, encouraging young Asian women to embrace their identities and celebrate their heritage.

Fatini is a freelance illustrator with a heart full of colour and a mind brimming with childhood memories. Her artistic journey began as art therapy through art journaling, fuelling her desire to experiment with various artistic streams to ensure her work remains fresh and engaging. With a deep foundation in art and design, she shapes her ability to translate emotions and experiences into captivating visuals.

Beyond commissioned projects, Fatini is a passionate self-publisher. Her book *Di Sebalik Tingkap*, explores themes of her life experiences, nostalgia, and the enduring power of childhood memories. Fatini is actively involved in local events and book illustration competitions in Malaysia. She was awarded the consolation prize in the Yusof Gajah Illustration Award at the Book Festival in 2023. In addition to books, she owns a small art business called NiniLukis, which offers merchandise based on local cultural visuals.

You can find us on Instagram:

@gutsyasian

www.ingramcontent.com/pod-product-compliance
Lightning Source LLC
Chambersburg PA
CBHW040950090526
44585CB00027BA/2886